NICKELODEON

ni hao, kai-lan

Happy Chinese New Year, Kai-lan!

adapted by Lauryn Silverhardt
based on the screenplay "Happy Chinese New Year!" written by Bradley Zweig
illustrated by Jason Fruchter and Aka Chikasawa

Simon Spotlight/Nickelodeon
New York   London   Toronto   Sydney

Kai-lan was getting ready for a very special day.

"*Ni hao!*" said Kai-lan. "Guess what? Today is a super special day! It's Chinese New Year! In Chinese, I say . . . *Xin nian kuai le!* Happy Chinese New Year! Did you know that red is a happy color?" asked Kai-lan. "That's why we wear red and hang red lanterns and red banners on Chinese New Year."

There was a knock at the door. Kai-lan's friends had arrived to help get ready for the celebration!

Kai-lan rushed downstairs and opened the door for her friends. Rintoo, Tolee, Hoho, and Lulu all came inside.

"Yes! I looove Chinese New Year!" exclaimed Rintoo.

"Me too!" cried Lulu. *"Xin nian kuai le!"*

Kai-lan added, "I love that on Chinese New Year, we get to spend the whole day with our family and friends!"

"Let's hang decorations for tonight's celebration," suggested Rintoo. "Great idea!" said Tolee.

Kai-lan and her friends got right to work. Tolee and Hoho hung red lanterns, while Kai-lan and Lulu hung banners.

As Rintoo put flowers on the table, something round caught his eye.

"Kai-lan, look what I found!" cried Rintoo. "A drum!"

"Do we get to play it?" asked Lulu.

"Everyone plays their drums during the parade," Kai-lan answered, "but you can try it out now."

Rintoo and Lulu started banging on the drum. They were having such a good time that they didn't notice when a dragon head appeared in the window!

"Look!" cried Tolee. "A dragon!"

"Don't worry, Tolee. It's not a real dragon!" said Kai-lan.

It was Kai-lan's grandpa, *YeYe*, wearing a dragon costume! Tolee was very relieved.

"I made this dragon costume for the parade," explained *YeYe*, as he pointed to the rest of the dragon costume that was spread out on the ground.

"I wish *we* could carry the dragon," said Rintoo.

"You can," said *YeYe*. "This year you are all old enough to carry the dragon!"

"Hooray!" said Kai-lan and her friends.

"But it's a big dragon," *YeYe* continued, "so you will have to work together as a team to carry it."

"We can work together!" exclaimed Tolee.

"Yeah!" added Kai-lan. "We're a Dragon Team!"

Rintoo was staring at the dragon, confused. "*YeYe*," he asked, "how do we know which part of the dragon to carry?"

"I'll show you," answered *YeYe*. "Everyone pick a Chinese number out of my hat, and then match it to the Chinese number on the side of the dragon."

Everyone took turns picking a card. Hoho picked first.

"I picked the number two! *Er!*" announced Hoho. Hoho found the Chinese number *er* near the head of the dragon.

"Wow," said Rintoo. "Hoho gets to be second in line."

Tolee picked next. He picked the number five. *Wu!* Tolee found his place next to the Chinese number *wu*.

"My job is to hold the tail!" exclaimed Tolee. "Nice to meet you, tail. *Ni hao!*"
"Hello, dragon tail!" Kai-lan laughed.

It was finally Rintoo's turn to pick a number. He picked the number three. *San!*

"Where's the number that looks like three?" asked Kai-lan.

When he saw he would be third in line, Rintoo looked disappointed. "My job is to hold the middle," Rintoo said, frowning.

Next it was Lulu's turn. She picked the number one. *Yi!* Lulu quickly found the match to her number.

"I'm the head of the dragon!" exclaimed Lulu.

"Aww," said Rintoo under his breath. "Lulu gets to be the head, and I'm stuck in the middle."

Kai-lan was the last person to pick a card. She picked the number four. *Si!* Kai-lan quickly found her place along the dragon.

"I'm between Rintoo and Tolee!" cried Kai-lan. "I like my job."

Everyone took their place by the dragon, lined up in order from numbers one through five: *yi*, *er*, *san*, *si*, *wu*.

It was time for the five friends to take their dragon to the Chinese New Year parade!

"Okay, everyone, when I count to three, lift up the dragon together," instructed *YeYe*. "Ready? *Yi . . . er . . . san!*"

They moved forward, and the dragon looked like it was walking all by itself. But after a few steps, the middle of the dragon started to sag. Rintoo looked very upset and dropped the middle of the dragon.

"I don't want to be the middle!" yelled Rintoo.

"We have a big problem," Tolee said. "Without Rintoo's help, the dragon falls down."

"And without Rintoo, we won't be able to carry the dragon in the Chinese New Year parade," added Lulu.

"But I don't want to be the middle!" cried Rintoo. "It's not an important job."

Kai-lan wanted to show Rintoo that every job on a team is important. She spotted a team of ants carrying a drumstick.

"Rintoo, look at the ant team," said Kai-lan. "The ants really know how to work together. Every ant is doing a super job."

Just then the middle ant let go of the drumstick to tie his shoelace.

The other ants struggled to keep the drumstick in the air! The middle ant quickly jumped back into place.

"Look," said Kai-lan. "Without the middle ant, the ant team almost dropped the drumstick."

"Wow," said Rintoo. "I guess the middle really *is* an important job."

"Every job on a team is super, super, super important!" exclaimed Kai-lan.

"The Dragon Team needs me!" cried Rintoo. "They really need me!"

He quickly found his place among his friends in the middle of the dragon.

"I'm sorry I let go of the dragon when you needed me to hold up the middle." Rintoo paused, then said, "And I'm glad to be back on the Dragon Team with all my friends!"

"The whole team is back together!" shouted Kai-lan as everyone cheered for Rintoo. "Come on, Dragon Team, let's go to the Chinese New Year parade!"

When they arrived at the Chinese New Year parade, everyone was wearing red clothes in honor of the happy day.

"Look," cried Hoho, pointing to the people in the crowd. "They are all wearing clothes that are red, *hong se*!"

Just then fireworks burst up above. "Oooh!" Lulu said, looking up at the sky. "The fireworks are all *hong se* too!"

Soon it was time for Kai-lan, Rintoo, Lulu, Tolee, and Hoho to do their dragon dance. "Let's go, Dragon Team!" shouted Kai-lan.

Everyone cheered as the Dragon Team moved the dragon through the parade, zigging and zagging together. They lifted the dragon up and down and made the dragon dance!

"This is awesome," shouted Rintoo. "I love being in the middle!"

After the Dragon Team finished their dance, Kai-lan and her friends all met up with *YeYe* in the garden for a big Chinese New Year dinner.

"Wonderful teamwork, everyone," *YeYe* said proudly. "It's time for our special dumplings!" *YeYe* announced as he placed a big bowl of dumplings on the table.

"Yummy!" exclaimed Tolee.

"Really yummy!" cried Hoho and Rintoo.

While everyone was eating, *YeYe* went inside and came out with a handful of red envelopes.

"Guess what?" asked *YeYe*. "I have something very special for everyone!"

"On Chinese New Year we get red envelopes," explained Kai-lan.

"And inside each envelope is something really special," said Rintoo.

"Wow, special coins!" exclaimed Tolee as he opened his envelope.

"Let's give a super special family hug to *YeYe*," suggested Kai-lan as her friends gathered around.

"Thank you, *YeYe*! Happy Chinese New Year!" they said together. "*Xin nian kuai le!*"

Kai-lan looked around at her grandpa and friends. "This was the best Chinese New Year ever because we were all together! You make my heart feel super happy!"